FOR DARBIE & JACK,

YOU BOTH ARE STRONGER THAN YOU'LL EVER
KNOW. MAY WHATEVER ROAD YOU CHOOSE BE
YOUR OWN.

Library of Congress-in-Publication Data is available upon request.

ISBN: 978-1-7366926-3-9 (hardcover)
ISBN: 978-1-7366926-2-2 (paperback)
ISBN: 978-1-7366926-1-5 (ebook)

Illustrations by Mag Takac

First printing edition 2021

RUN REBEL RUN

WRITTEN BY PETER MATKIWSKY
ILLUSTRATED BY MAG TAKAC

My name is Rebel
But sometimes mom calls me hun

SHE TELLS ME MY DREAMS CAN BE
WHAT LIFE HAS TO COME

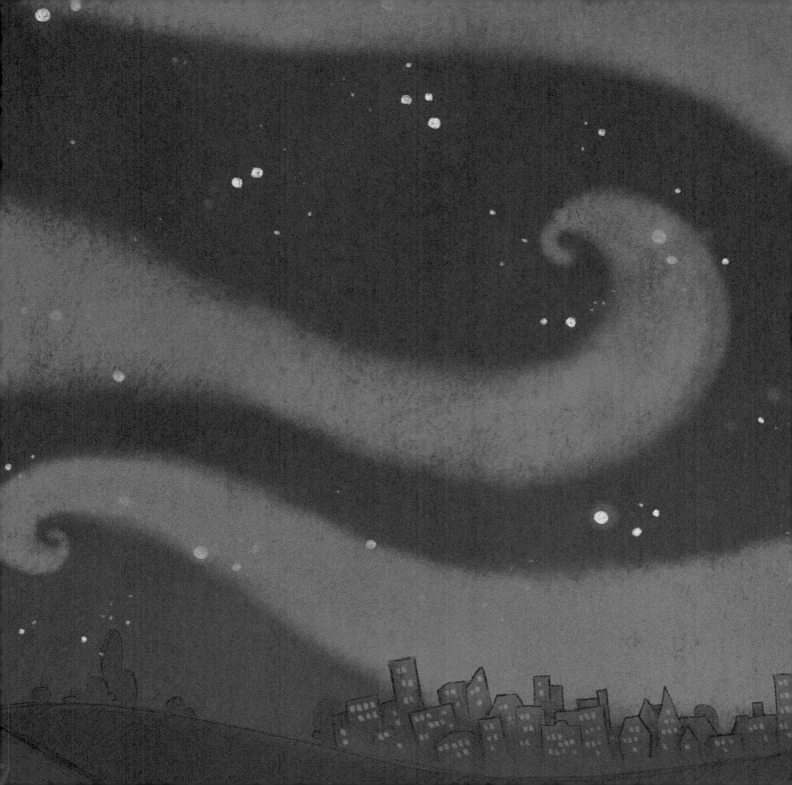

JUST SAY THEM OUT LOUD
SO THE UNIVERSE'S WEAVE CAN BE SPUN

THEN GO CHASE THEM DOWN
AND REMEMBER TO RUN

THE ROAD MAY HAVE BUMPS
BUT EVEN THEY CAN BE FUN

BUT NOT ALL THE MOMENTS
WILL BE AS PLEASANT AS SOME

SO WHEN THE JOURNEY GETS HARD
AND PRESSURE FEELS LIKE A TON

SOME FRIENDS MAY SAY
THAT YOUR DREAMS ARE DUMB

BUT DREAMS TAKE TIME
SO THEY SHOULD GET NONE

PLUS PLENTY OF PEOPLE
LIVE UNDER THE SUN

AND WHO NEEDS A FRIEND
WHO'S A NEGATIVE ONE

IF YOU HAVE DOUBTS
THAT MAKE YOU FEEL GLUM

JUST KNOW THAT THOSE FEELINGS
HAPPEN TO EVERYONE

HAVING FAITH YOU WILL MAKE IT,
SHOULD BE YOUR ONE RULE OF THUMB

SO BELIEVE IN YOURSELF
AND RUN REBEL RUN

YOU MAY WANT TO WISH REAL LOUD
LIKE A DRUM

BUT DON'T TALK TOO MUCH,
FOR THERE'S THINGS TO GET DONE

AND IF YOU SHOULD FAIL
AND FEEL SUDDENLY NUMB

YOU'LL BE TEMPTED TO QUIT
BUT TRY NOT TO SUCCUMB

EVERY FAILURE'S A LESSON
THAT YOU CAN LEARN FROM

SO KEEP ON TRYING,
YOU'LL NEED THE WISDOM

NO NEED FOR SHORTCUTS
OFFERED BY WICKED ONES

ALWAYS STAY ON YOUR GRIND
AND FIGHT FOR EACH CRUMB

BUT ALWAYS BE KIND
REMEMBER WHERE YOU CAME FROM

JUST PUT IN THE WORK
AND TRUST YOU'LL OVERCOME

FOR ALL OF YOUR EFFORTS
WILL ADD UP TO THE SUM

NOW LOOK IN THE MIRROR
TO SEE WHAT YOU'VE BECOME

YOU'VE DONE IT, HOORAY!
YOU'VE FINALLY WON

BUT THIS ISN'T THE END,
YOUR STORY'S ONLY BEGUN

I KNEW YOU COULD DO IT,
NOW RUN REBEL RUN

THE END.